A gift for: ______________________________

From: ___________________________________

One Small Donkey

A Division of Thomas Nelson Publishers

For Ellie, Cassie, and Maddie:
Never forget that you can do all things through
Christ, who gives you strength (Philippians 4:13).

One Small Donkey

Published in Nashville, Tennessee, by Tommy Nelson. Tommy Nelson is an imprint of Thomas Nelson. Thomas Nelson is a registered trademark of HarperCollins Christian Publishing, Inc.

Illustrated by Marta Álvarez Miguéns

Tommy Nelson titles may be purchased in bulk for educational, business, fund-raising, or sales promotional use. For information, please e-mail SpecialMarkets@ThomasNelson.com.

ISBN-13: 978-0-7180-8747-0

Library of Congress Cataloging-in-Publication Data is on file.

Printed in China

16 17 18 19 20 LEO 6 5 4 3 2

Mfr: LEO / Heshan, China / December 2016 / PO # 9424184

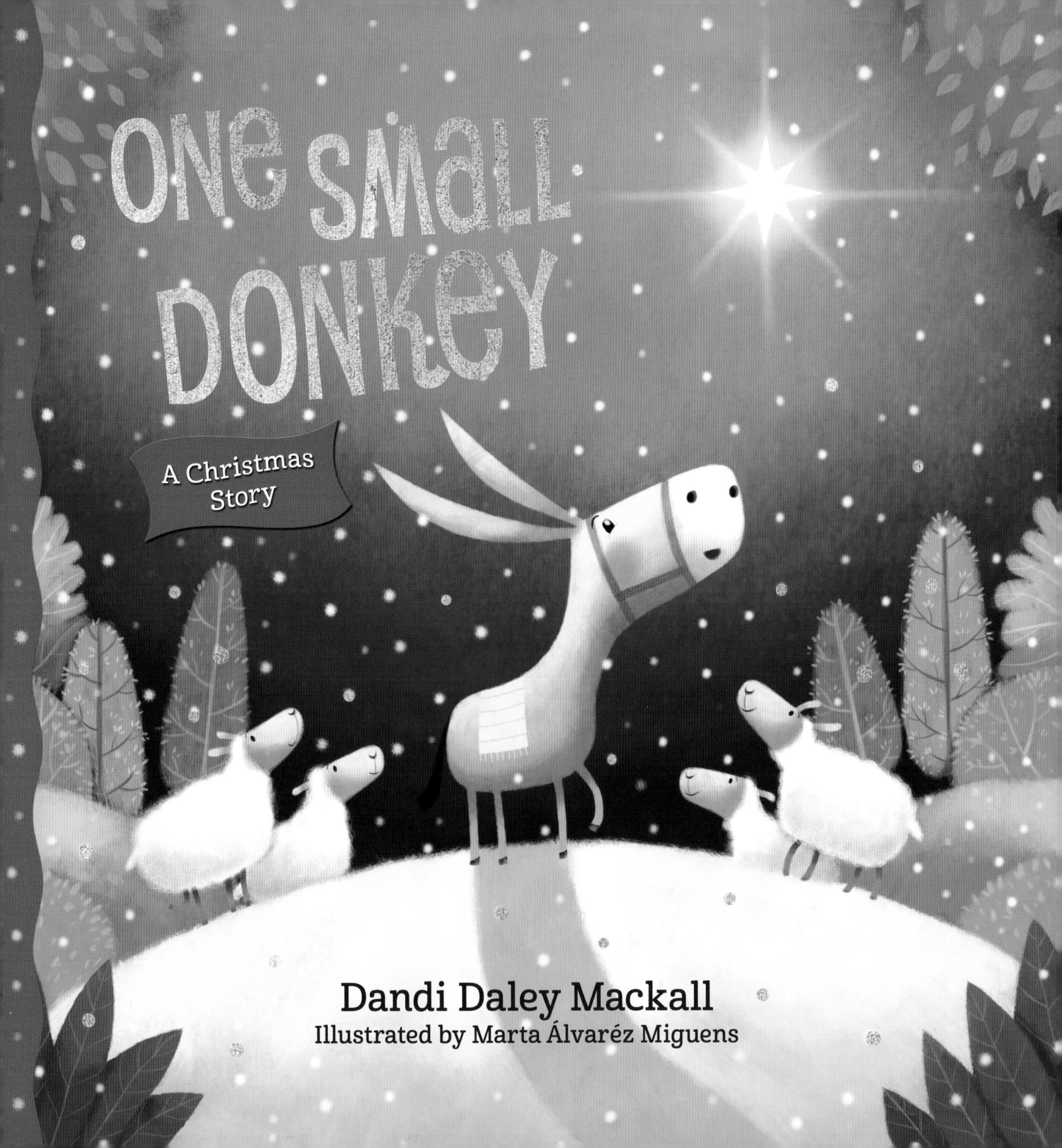
One Small Donkey
A Christmas Story
Dandi Daley Mackall
Illustrated by Marta Álvaréz Miguens

The inspiration for *One Small Donkey* came last Christmas Eve. Our neighbors in rural Ohio are Amish, and we passed a buggy pulled by the smallest horse. But that little guy was speeding in the snow. Our granddaughter Ellie, then five years old, and I had been having a heart-to-heart about her need to be bold and volunteer for things in kindergarten, even though she was the smallest kid in the class. We passed that little horse at exactly the right time. Though the Bible doesn't mention whether a donkey carried Mary to Bethlehem, one thing is certain: even the littlest ones can do big things for God.

Dandi Daley Mackall

One small donkey on a lonely hill,
Hunting for a blade of grass,
Sees big horses full of power and might,
Prancing proudly as they pass.

One small donkey wishes he were big,
Marching on a festive day,
Stallions lining up to follow him,
Knowing he will lead the way.

One small donkey hears his master call:
"Come along! It's time to go."
Donkey, rushing to his master's voice,
Wishes he were not so slow.

One small donkey holding very still—
Joseph ties the journey pack.
Mary, grinning, though she's great with child,
Climbs upon the donkey's back.

One small donkey with a *clip, clip, clop*,
Trots along the winding road,
Hurries on the trail to Bethlehem,
Mindful of his priceless load.

One small donkey underneath the stars
Senses the Creator's hand.
Pure, white snowflakes soon begin to fall,
Whitening the Promised Land.

One small donkey hears a *baa, baa, baa*.
Shepherds watch their flocks by night.
Fancy horses rear and pass them by.
Up above, one star shines bright.

One small donkey at the city gate,
Bumped and shoved and pushed aside.
Joseph *knock*, *knock*, *knocks* on every door,
Seeking shelter for his bride.

One small donkey knows the time is near.
Joseph says, “We’ll go down there.”
Just a stable for the soldiers’ steeds?
Nothing but a manger bare.

One small donkey who does not fit in,
Not with horses sleek and strong—
Mary strokes his head then settles in.
Donkey knows it won't be long.

One small donkey hears a baby cry.
Joseph gives a shout for joy:
"God has sent His only Son to us,
Jesus—precious little boy!"

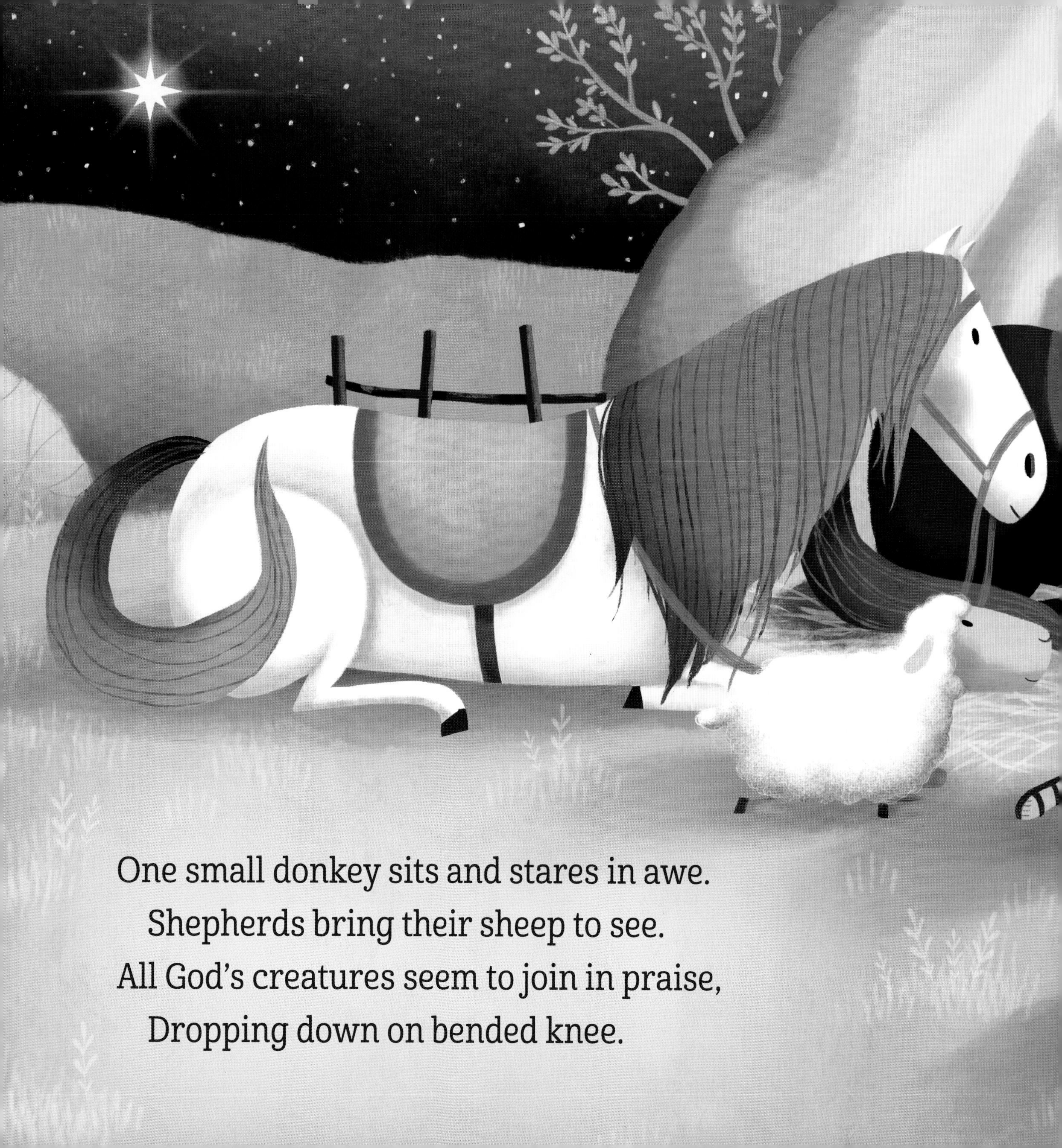

One small donkey sits and stares in awe.
Shepherds bring their sheep to see.
All God's creatures seem to join in praise,
Dropping down on bended knee.

One small donkey with a *hee-hee-haw*!
Cheering at the Savior's birth—
One small donkey with a giant heart
Welcomes Christ, our peace on earth.